www.mascotbooks.com

Barbara the Bunny and the International Lovie Network

For more information, please contact:
Mascot Books
620 Herndon Parkway, Suite 320
Herndon, VA 20170
info@mascotbooks.com

Library of Congress Control Number: 2021909858

CPSIA Code: PRT1021A

ISBN-13: 978-1-64543-928-8

Printed in the United States

For my family.
XO, JBL.

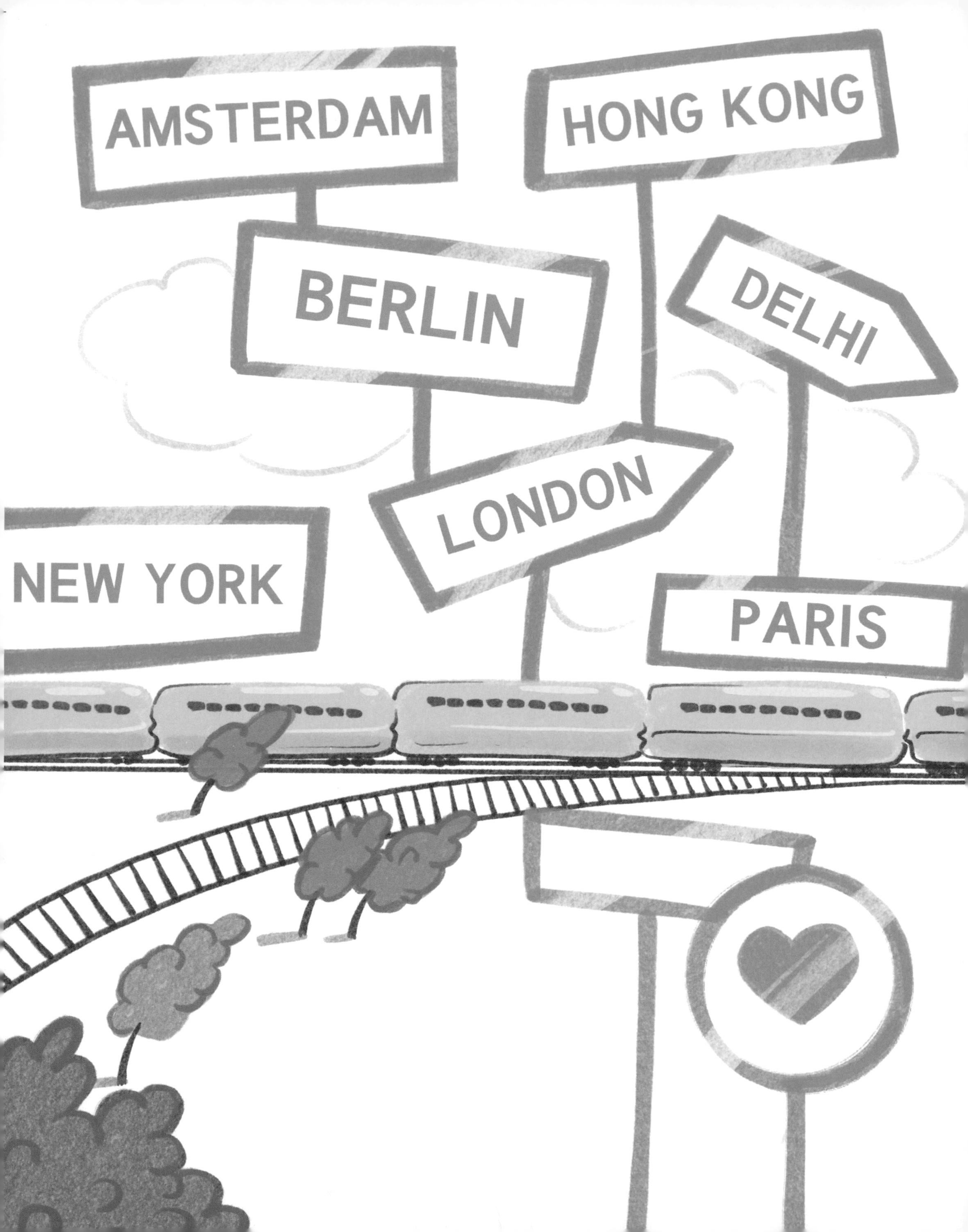
AMSTERDAM
HONG KONG
BERLIN
DELHI
LONDON
NEW YORK
PARIS

BARBARA THE BUNNY

and the
INTERNATIONAL LOVIE NETWORK

Jennifer Lavelle

Illustrated by **Irina Kudria**

SOME BUNNY
LOVES YOU!
XO,
Jenlavelle

Not many people are aware, you know,
that there is a place where only Lovies go.
Ever misplace your Teddy, even just for a while?
He might be out on official business, Lovie style.

When a child needs a Lovie less and less,
they often help with official Lovie business.
With so much more time on their paws,
why not help a worthy cause?

Barbara the Bunny's matted
fur was a badge of pride.
It was her honor to be by
her Boy's side.

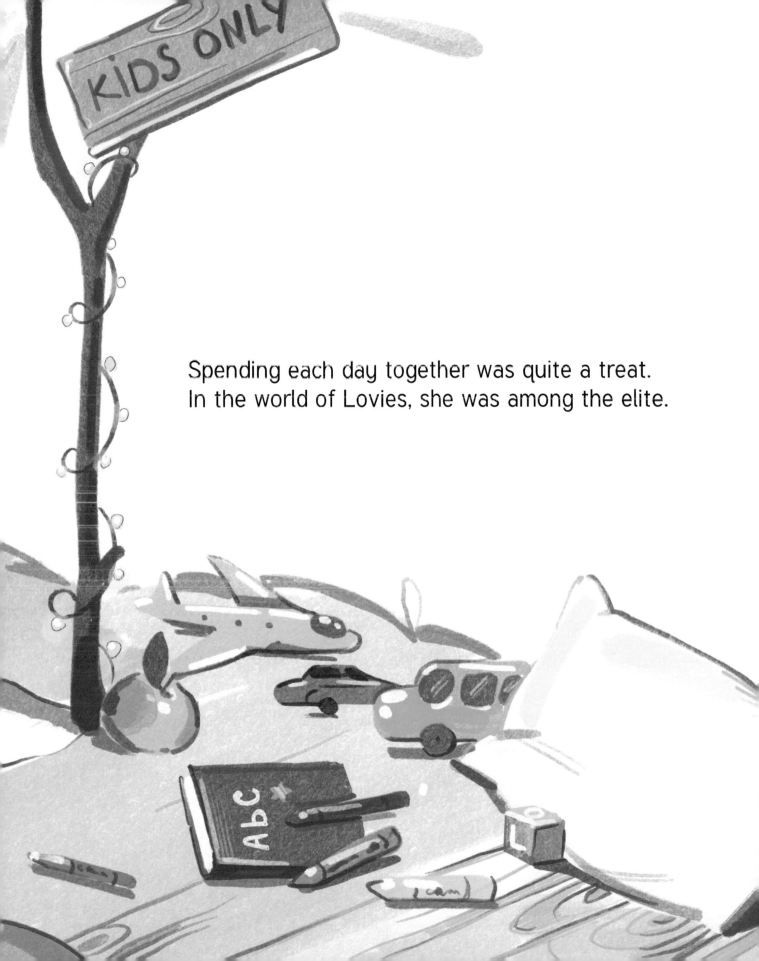

Spending each day together was quite a treat.
In the world of Lovies, she was among the elite.

The International Lovie Network was a legendary team,
and becoming a member was any Lovies' dream.
But while the ILN did help Lovies in need,
Barbara believed it wasn't her speed.

Of course, Boy left each day for school,
and she couldn't join him when he played in the pool . . .
Still, Barbara just couldn't imagine being away from her Boy.
She was so much more than just another toy.

One day, as Barbara flopped on the stairs,
she heard the "click-clack" of the shoes Mama wears.
Mama told the Boy he'd visit his Grandma Mimi TODAY!
He couldn't wait to see her and play!

As the Boy skipped out, happily screaming,
Barbara watched from the steps, beaming.
"A ride in a car and a plane! Won't this be great?
I love adventures with my amazing playmate!"

Suddenly, the Boy ran off without a care.
Barbara sat waiting on the bottom stair.
She thought to herself, *They'll soon be back.*
They'll grab me, and I'll ride in Boy's pack.

So, Barbara waited and waited.
For hours, she hesitated and debated . . .
Until finally, she thought, *This just can't be!*
How could Boy forget about ME?

She didn't want to make a fuss,
but had she been cast aside like that old turtle, Gus?
She hadn't seen Gus since he'd been thrown on the shelf.
Barbara decided she'd just have to find the Boy herself.

She called the only group up to the task:
the ILN! All it took was a simple ask.

A whole gang of SEALs arrived in a special contraption:
a tiny plane designed for Lovie extraction.
"Hurry, get in!" Barbara heard the commander bark.
With seatbelts fastened, they flew out of park.

The ILN didn't disappoint:
in minutes, they reached the Lovie Launch Point.

Helicopters, trains, buses, and planes
all for Lovies . . . it's hard to explain!

Each ILN operative is ever-ready to respond,
to support and defend a very special bond:
the connection each Lovie has with their child.
That's a love worth protecting, no matter how wild.

As the flight flew on, Barbara kicked up her feet.
She had no idea she was in for a treat:
fun bubble baths for the whole crew!
Barbara was back to looking good as new.

Soon, all the Lovies were spotless and clean.
Washed and brushed, Barbara felt like a queen.
With everyone ready, they prepared for landing.
The ILN had been truly outstanding.

Barbara, so excited, jumped off the plane,
so happy she had no bags to claim.

She hopped to the waiting Lovie Bus,
thinking, *A seat near a window is always a plus.*

And who did she see driving that bus?
None other than that OLD TURTLE, GUS!
They smiled for nearly a minute straight,
until Gus said, "Hop in, Babs, we're gonna be late!"

After a full day of travel, Barbara rounded the bend
on a bus packed full of new Lovie friends.
The Boy was playing outside the front door.
When he saw Barbara, he felt his heart soar.

He squeezed her so tight, she thought she'd explode—
a great big hug after much time on the road.

The International Lovie Network—the ILN.
Barbara could feel herself starting to grin.
She was sure a new adventure was about to begin.

About the Author

Jennifer Lavelle earned an advertising degree at Southern Methodist University while on scholarship for swimming. After holding several advertising positions and starting Mizzen+Main with her husband, she became a full-time mother to two amazing children. Jennifer currently works as a children's author, and she enjoys delighting children through imagination and storytelling each and every day. She lives in Dallas, Texas, with her husband, children, and two big red dogs.

About the Illustrator

Irina Kudria is a children's book illustrator based in Ukraine. She has been passionate about illustration since early childhood, which led her to turn it into a career. Now, Irina's work is concentrated on creating unique books to help young readers start the lifetime journey of exploring the world and its beauty.